BOBCAT

NORTH AMERICA'S CAT

STEPHEN R. SWINBURNE

BOYDS MILLS PRESS

For Susan Morse, who works every day to save habitat for
bobcats and other wild creatures.

—S. R. S.

Acknowledgments: Many thanks to Kim Royar, wildlife biologist, and Susan Morse, habitat specialist and
wildlife tracker, for their help reviewing the manuscript.
Photographs: Stephen R. Swinburne: Pages: 4, 7, 8, 9 (top right), 13, 15, 17, 18, 19, 21, 22, 23 (left), 24, 25;
Susan Morse: Jacket photo and pages: 1, 3, 6, 9 (left), 10, 11, 12, 14, 16, 20, 23 (right), 26, 27, 28, 31, 32;
Library of Congress: Page 30; Vermont Historical Society: page 29; Reed Prescott III,
illustrator; concept by Susan Morse: Page 27

Text copyright © 2001 by Stephen R. Swinburne

Photographs copyright © 2001 by Stephen R. Swinburne, except where noted

Published by Caroline House
Boyds Mills Press, Inc.
A Highlights Company
815 Church Street
Honesdale, Pennsylvania 18431
Printed in China

U.S. Cataloging-in-Publication Data
    (Library of Congress Standards)

Bobcat : North America's cat / written and photographed by
Stephen R. Swinburne. –1st ed.
[32]p. : col. Ill. ;   cm.
Includes index.
Summary: An examination of bobcats, their behavior and habitat.
ISBN 1-56397-843-1
1. Bobcat. I. Title.
599.75/ 36 -dc21   2001   AC   CIP
00-102352

First edition, 2001
Book designed by Tim Gillner
The text of this book is set in 13-point Garamond Book.

10 9 8 7 6 5 4 3 2 1

CONTENTS

Prologue

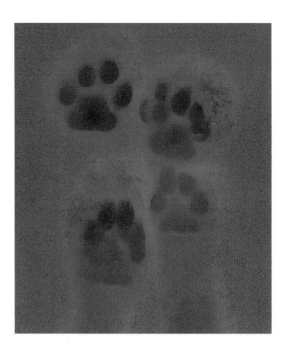

On a frosty winter afternoon in Vermont, I find a set of tracks at the base of a rugged wall of rock. Each track is a circle of four toe prints and a palm pad. They look old in the icy crust, as if the animal that made them had once walked through fresh snow leaving its tracks frozen and perfect. Who walked here? I try to put the clues together. The tracks are about 15 inches apart, a little small for a coyote and too big for a house cat. I'm walking among rocky ledges in woods a mile from any road. Are these bobcat tracks? I've always wanted to get a good look at a wild bobcat. This could be my chance.

I follow the trail of prints another ten feet. They suddenly stop. The tracks vanish. Maybe the animal jumped, so I search the ground to see if I can pick up the trail. I look everywhere but can't find another track. I lean against the cliff. I'm stumped. I look up. Ledges and rocky perches cover the face of the cliff. Only a bobcat could move in that terrain and disappear so completely. I imagine the bobcat jumping to the ledge above my head just as easily as my cat springs to the kitchen counter. Dogs can't jump like that. Cats could teach Michael Jordan a thing or two about jumping.

BOBCAT FACTS

Where does the name bobcat *come from? Most cats have long tails, but the bobcat's tail is only 5 to 6 inches long. The bobcat looks as if someone cut off or "bobbed" its tail (the lynx's tail is even shorter.) The bobcat's tail is striped, and its tip is black on the top and white underneath. Bobcats have white spots that really stand out on the backs of their ears. These spots and the white tip of the tail help kittens follow their mother even at night.*

Bobcat's tail

White spots on the bobcat's ears

I didn't see the bobcat. In fact, I've seen a bobcat in the wild only once. I've photographed captive bobcats in Idaho, watched bobcats doze in the sun in a New York City zoo as airplanes roared overhead, and tracked bobcats in the back-woods of New England. My only sighting of a wild bobcat was brief but memorable. I was driving through Vermont one evening when I passed a bobcat sitting beside the edge of the road. For a long moment, I watched this wild and beautiful creature in the glare of my lights. It looked as at home in the night woods as stars do in the sky. I braked and backed up slowly to get a better look, but the cat was gone.

Bobcats are masters at hiding and sitting still. They have more patience than the Great Sphinx. I've found their tracks, a scent post, their scat, and their resting spots. I've even found where they've made a kill. But bobcats are shy and secretive. Even biologists who study bobcats rarely see them. Bobcats hunt mostly at night but can be active at any time of the day. A spotted, dappled coat helps the cat blend in with its background. Bobcats are perfectly camouflaged. Large, furry paws make the bobcat as silent as a forest ghost.

Could the bobcat whose tracks I've followed be long gone? Or is it right now tucked into a sunny ledge fifty feet above my head? If I were a bobcat, I'd be perched in a cozy nook, soaking up the last rays of this winter sunshine. I scan the whole cliff with my binoculars until I'm chilled to the bone.

I head home feeling thrilled and lucky to have found a trace of the mysterious wildcat. When you go looking for bobcats, any sign is a good sign.

Chapter One

A Cat Is Not a Dog

I'M SITTING THREE FEET FROM A BOBCAT. The only thing between us is a straw-thin, chain link fence. The cat doesn't trust me. I don't trust the cat.

On a cold winter day, I've come to pay my respects to the resident bobcat at Trevor Zoo on the campus of Millbrook Preparatory School in upstate New York. Although it's a small zoo, more than 120 animals are on display, including the endangered red wolf. The cool thing about this zoo is that the high school students help run the place.

I'm visiting this captive bobcat because it's not easy to get close to a wild one. I want to learn how a bobcat moves, how it reacts to sounds and sights. I want to see it eat. After watching this bobcat for over an hour, I've decided that if you want to get an idea of how a bobcat behaves, watch your cat. The behaviors of a bobcat and a house cat are amazingly similar.

My cat, Boo, is a small black cat. She is graceful and independent. Boo spends most of her waking hours trying to accomplish the major goal in her life: being comfortable. I look into her olive-yellow eyes and imagine her dreaming about kitty treats and full bowls of milk. There's definitely a wilder creature behind the golden-yellow stare of the ten-year-old bobcat I'm watching, but all the same, a cat's a cat.

When I first arrive at the zoo, the bobcat dozes in his hay-lined box perched in the corner of the cage. He doesn't budge until Jennifer, one of the zoo's assistants, rubs a sprig of catnip against the fence. The bobcat slowly emerges, yawning and stretching, nonchalantly sniffs the catnip, and flumps down against the fence, cautiously eyeing me. Jennifer says she'll get some food and tells me not to get close to the fence. "He'll reach through and claw you," she warns.

The cat doesn't move until Jennifer returns with a dead rat. She uses a long metal arm to place the rat inside the cage. When the metal arm is retracted, the bobcat grabs the rat in its mouth, carrying it to the other side of the cage. I listen to soft bone-crunching bites as the bobcat begins gobbling the rat's head. With its head to one side, the bobcat uses the sharp teeth called carnassial teeth in the rear of its mouth to scissor-cut swallowable chunks of meat. Bobcats have twenty-eight teeth, including four sharp canines for puncturing and gripping. The cat gobbles the rat in a minute; only the tail remains.

Bobcats range in color from tawny to reddish to more gray in winter.

The Trevor Zoo cat finishes his meal.

BOBCAT FACTS

Adult bobcats live alone. They seek company from late February to early April when male bobcats search for females. Each male might mate with a number of females. After mating, females look for a den where they can give birth.

Males play no part in raising the young. Bobcats prefer small caves, rocky ledges, overhangs, boulder piles, or hollow trees as den sites. A secluded, secret spot high up and out of the way provides safety from hungry coyotes and other predators. In spring, two to three kittens are born. The eyes of the kittens are tightly closed, and they open nine to ten days after birth.

Bobcat kittens are totally helpless and depend on their mother for food. At about six weeks, the kittens are old enough to venture from the den and explore. By fall or early winter, the young bobcats leave their mother for good.

A rocky ledge is perfect bobcat habitat.

If you want to appreciate a carnivore, watch a cat eat its prey. Bobcats in the wild work harder for their food than this caged cat, of course. Wild bobcats use stealth to stalk and ambush their prey. They need protective cover, such as tall grass or bushes, to hide. They are also masters of patience and can crouch for hours in one spot, ready to pounce on prey. A cat will wait on a rocky ledge, crouched low, slowly scanning the terrain for any sign of movement. If it spots something, the cat slinks to the ground and patiently stalks closer. When it gets within ten yards of the prey, the bobcat rushes to attack. Powerful hind legs act like a spring, giving the cat a faster start than its prey. Cats have small hearts, making them sprinters, not long-distance runners. After a chase, a bobcat may need ten minutes or more to catch its breath. About 20 to 30 percent of their attacks are successful.

The bobcat must hunt in order to survive. Amazing eyesight and acute hearing help the wild cat hunt efficiently. If a human can see in dim light, bobcats can see in light that is six times dimmer. They can swivel their ears very quickly to pinpoint the faintest sound. And their ear tufts are antennae that detect the source of a sound. Bobcats have ¾-inch-long razor-sharp claws on their front feet. These daggers pin down prey while the bobcat kills its victim with a bite. The bobcat's two dozen long whiskers are specialized hairs that help aim the cat's mouth for a quick-killing bite.

Bobcats are nocturnal animals but are often most active around dawn and dusk. Unlike my cat, a bobcat is not fussy about what it eats. Bobcats prefer rabbits and hares, but they are opportunists and will eat whatever is easy to catch:

Cats have incredible patience. They can wait for hours, conserving energy, and then pounce.

BOBCAT FACTS

The place where a bobcat hunts, mates, and rests is called its territory. Bobcats mark their territories using scent and visual signs. They make scent posts by spraying urine on rotting stumps. They cover up their droppings or deposit their feces, or scat, out in the open or along a path in "scratches" and "scrapes."

Bobcats will also rake trees with their claws to leave scent from glands between their toes. These signs are enough to warn off any bobcat entering another's territory. If two bobcats meet, they may fight. Fighting bobcats make all sorts of sounds, including meows, growls, hisses, spits, and snarls.

Scrape

Scat

muskrats, squirrels, mice, beavers, opossums, insects, and birds. They can also kill larger animals, such as white-tailed deer that are bedded down. Bobcat researcher Susan Morse says bobcats have an easier time making a killing bite to the throat if the deer is lying down. She has found four deer killed by bobcats in the mountains near her farm in northern Vermont.

Given enough food, cover, and protection from people, bobcats can live just about anywhere. They are truly North America's cat and are found in every state with the possible exception of Delaware. Their range extends from southern Canada all the way to central Mexico. Their northern neighbor, the lynx, has a range that covers most of Canada,

Current Bobcat Range

northern Europe, and Asia. Bobcats are very adaptable and survive in lots of habitats. They live in areas as diverse as mountain forests, deserts, swamps, and evergreen and deciduous forests. Bobcats are found even along the edges of farms and the suburbs of cities, although the latter is not good habitat for them. Unlike the omnivorus coyote that can eat plants and garbage in urban and suburban areas, the bobcat may not always find enough prey to survive in those places.

The bobcat I'm watching at the Trevor Zoo was born August 14, 1990. This bobcat's father lived till he was twenty-one years old. Son and father bobcat shared the same cage until the father died in January 2000. Most bobcats in the wild live ten to twelve years. Life as a predator is hard. Mountain lions and wolves kill adult bobcats; and great horned owls, foxes, dogs, and coyotes kill kittens. Bobcats chased by dogs escape by climbing trees.

Zoos are great places for many reasons, including seeing wildlife up close. But it is important to maintain wild bobcat populations in their natural habitat.

The Trevor Zoo bobcat doesn't have to worry about mountain lions, yapping dogs, or lean, cruel winters. In the last hour this bobcat has had mouse for an appetizer, followed by two large rats. As the bobcat waddles back to the box in the corner of the cage, its fat belly brushes the ground. The cat curls up in the warm hay, and its eyes squeeze shut in contentment. The cat is asleep. If captive bobcats can be happy, the Trevor Zoo bobcat is one happy cat.

Chapter Two

BOBCATS DON'T EAT PIZZA

"WELCOME TO RABBIT HEAVEN!" says Alcott Smith. I'm standing with eight other naturalists on a low hill overlooking the wide marshes at the headwaters of Lake Champlain in Vermont. Lake Champlain is the seventh-largest freshwater lake in the United States. I look west to New York and see the foothills of the Adirondack Mountains. Blackberry thickets, small shrubs, and lots of open, sunny patches make this perfect rabbit habitat. What makes this rabbit heaven also makes this bobcat heaven.

"Bobcats love eating rabbit," says Smith, a retired veterinarian and tracking expert. On a brilliant blue-sky morning in early February, our group, with Alcott in the lead, sets off on a search for bobcat sign.

Bobcats prey on many kinds of rabbits, including Eastern cottontail, snowshoe hare, and white-tailed jack rabbit. Here a bobcat feasts on a snowshoe hare.

We haven't gone far before I find a maze of tracks criss-crossing under a tangle of blackberry brambles. I'm pretty sure they're rabbit tracks. The tips of the blackberry plants end in neat 45-degree angles. Rabbits have very sharp top and bottom front teeth, slicing perfect angle cuts on the plants they browse. This is a good sign. Where there are rabbits, often there are bobcats.

Near the blackberry brambles, Alcott finds the first bobcat track of the day. The midday sun is melting the snow. It's not a perfect track, but Alcott points out the round shape, the palm pad, and four toes. And there are no claw marks. Cats retract their claws when walking or running, so claw marks rarely show up in tracks. Cats use their claws to make kills. They need to keep them in good shape. The tracks of dogs, coyotes, and wolves most often differ from cats because they show their nail marks

Twenty feet from the first bobcat track, Alcott stops two tufts of windblown rabbit fur tumbling across the surface of

BOBCAT FACTS

Bobcat track: *The big difference between a cat track and a dog track is that the bobcat print is round and the coyote or dog track is oval. Bobcat tracks show four toes in a circular print with a rear palm pad. The claws do not show. The track is about 2 inches long by 2 inches wide.*

Cottontail rabbit track: *A rabbit track has two small front tracks, one in front of the other, while the back-feet tracks are side by side ahead of the front tracks.*

Squirrel track: *A squirrel track is very similar to the rabbit's except that the squirrel's two small front tracks are side by side.*

Bobcats love rocky ledges as lookouts for hunting and as sunning spots.

We found where a bobcat had fed on a rabbit.

the snow. He holds them up for us to see. He turns 360 degrees, scanning for any sign of a kill site.

"There's probably a bobcat kill nearby," he says. "Cats will sometimes cache or bury their prey under leaves, snow, weeds, or whatever is available. They even use their prey's fur." If a bobcat kills a large animal and doesn't eat all of it, the cat caches the prey, returning later to feed.

We don't find the bobcat kill, but we do see further sign of the mysterious cats. Along the edge of a rocky wall, in a shallow pocket in the cliff, we find where a bobcat fed on a rabbit. Alcott points out scattered, bleached-white bones on the floor of the overhang.

Further along the cliff face, under another rocky overhang, Alcott discovers a bobcat day bed, or lay. Like house cats, bobcats spend a lot of time resting and sleeping during the day. They seek a sheltered spot along a steep hillside or cliff. They like places with good views. Here they rest and can scan the surrounding countryside for any moving prey. If they spot something, they slink down from the ledge to stalk the prey.

I hug the rock wall and inch out to get a better look at the cat's resting spot. I pull myself up and peek into the cozy nook. I can see where the cat made a soft bed of dry grass and wilted brown ferns in the center of the flat ledge. I reach up and put my hand in the middle of the bed. For an instant, I connect with this wild creature. I turn and look out from my rocky perch and try to imagine this view through a bobcat's eyes.

Our group descends the snow-covered hillside, zigzagging back and forth. Some of us head straight down by sliding on our bottoms. As we pick our way down to the base of the steep, rock-strewn hillside, I look up and think about what an inhospitable place this is for people; but for a cat it's heaven.

"I think I've found our kitty friend," says Alcott, pointing with his walking stick to a set of tracks descending from the hill. "This is the route the bobcat took from his rocky perch to the marsh down here to hunt." I stare at the soft-edged holes and have a hard time turning them into bobcat tracks. But Alcott is not finished reading the story in the snow. A fallen tree over a jumble of rocks at the forest edge caught the bobcat's eye.

"Do you see how the bobcat avoided the deep snow around the boulders and tightrope-walked across this downed tree?" Alcott says. Given a choice, cats will usually walk on a log or a downed tree. Once elevated, they look down on unsuspecting mice scurrying from the log. All of us smile because we, too, are beginning to read the story the bobcat left us. I follow the bobcat's trail across the snow-

Here a bobcat avoided deep snow by walking across this downed tree.

NATURE DICTIONARY

ambush: *to hide and then attack prey animal*

cache: *a hidden supply of food, such as a dead deer or rabbit*

canine teeth: *the pointed teeth on each side of the upper and lower jaws*

captivity: *holding an animal that is not wild or free in an enclosed area*

carnivore: *an animal that eats the flesh of its prey*

deciduous: *a tree that sheds its leaves in the autumn, unlike an evergreen*

feces: *the droppings or body wastes of an animal*

felid: *a member of the cat family*

habitat: *the natural environment of a plant or animal that provides food, water, shelter, and space for it to survive*

nocturnal: *active at night*

sign: *the track, scent, or presence left by an animal*

spinal cord: *a thick cord of nerves along the backbone*

stalk: *to hunt an animal by sneaking up on it in a quiet, secret way*

tufts: *a bunch of hair that grows at one end and sticks out*

The bobcat tracks led me to a urine-scented stump.

covered log, to its leap to the forest floor, where it stopped to spray a stump, and then out along the marsh to hunt.

We track the cat's footprints along the tree line at the edge of the marsh. After a quarter of a mile or so, animal traffic at the marsh's edge increases. We cross muskrat tracks and turkey tracks. We see small piles of fresh wood chips at the base of a dead tree. A pileated woodpecker had chiseled into the bark, searching for ants.

Winter days end early, and we have a long walk back to our cars. In the last bit of evening light, we find where the bobcat has made a kill. In a patch of scarlet snow we make out the bloody remains of a muskrat, partially buried under snow and leaves. We can't read the whole story in the fading light, but the cat found what it came looking for. Across the marsh, cattails shiver in a gust of wind. A sliver of moon sinks in the west. Somewhere out there bobcats move between the shadows.

Chapter Three

SIXTH-GRADE SLEUTHS SEARCH FOR SIGN

ON A MILD MARCH DAY with the last scraps of winter on the ground, I tag along as Mr. Rampone and Mrs. Hunt's sixth-grade classes from Mettawee Community School in Pawlet, Vermont, go looking for bobcat sign. Chris Alexopoulos, a wildlife biologist with the U.S. Forest Service, leads the outing to a nearby nature preserve.

The kids pour out of the yellow school bus parked on a muddy road inside the preserve. Chris hoists up his mounted bobcat and gathers everyone around to check it out.

"Wow, cool cat!" one of the kids says.

"Awesome face," says another.

Chris asks what are important features of good bobcat habitat. Like a well-rehearsed chorus, the group chimes, "Ledges, wetlands, and lots of rabbits and deer."

The sixth-grade class from the Mettawee Community School in Pawlet, Vermont

The sixth graders get a look at a mounted bobcat.

I stand on the edge of the group listening to the ring of children, impressed by how much these kids know about bobcats. As we break into smaller groups, Chris fills me in on what they've studied.

The sixth-grade classes at Mettawee are taking part in a program called "Bobcats in a Changing Landscape." The bobcat unit is part of a larger science study called "Environmental Citizenship," which is offered by the Vermont Institute of Natural Science. The kids are well versed in the world of bobcats.

We plunge into the woods with eyes peeled for animal sign. We soon find deer tracks in a patch of frozen snow.

"Hey, deer tracks look like little hearts!" says one of the kids. Chris reminds everyone that where there are deer, there may be bobcat.

We find deer tracks in the icy crust. The white-tailed deer is one of North America's most abundant large animals. The bobcat is its natural enemy.

While we all get a good look at the deer prints, Chris explains that New England bobcats occasionally depend on deer in the winter. On average, during the winter, a bobcat can eat at least three deer. A large animal, such as a dead deer, may provide the carnivorous bobcat with enough food for weeks in the winter. Not far from where we find the tracks, Chris shows us a pile of deer bones beside a large maple tree. He says he found them last year and this may have been the work of a bobcat.

One of the students finds a turkey feather. We learn that wild turkey is definitely on the bobcat menu. We break out of the woods, entering a wide field. Gangs of crows fill the morning silence with their raucous calls: "Caw! Caw!" On the far side of the field, the woods angle sharply up into a steep hill. Rocky ledges cover the top half of the hill.

Bobcat feeding on a wild turkey

What a perfect place to hang out if you were a bobcat! Bobcats will use those ledges as a lookout for hunting as well as a sunny spot to stay warm in the winter. A female could find a den in those rocks. Her kittens would be safe up there.

Some of the kids walk over to the base of the hill to explore for bobcat tracks. Chris and I and the remaining students prowl along the edge of the field, looking for sign. We haven't gone far when we hear one of the kids calling us over.

"Wow, look at this!" shouts one of the boys. "It's a dead rabbit."

One boy found a turkey feather and some deer bones— evidence that bobcat may be in the area.

Bobcats kill rabbits by sinking their canine teeth into the animal's neck and cutting the spinal cord.

"This is great," says Chris. "Be careful not to disturb anything. We want to figure out what happened here if we can."

A few of us gather around to inspect the scene. We look for clues that might tell us who killed this cottontail rabbit. The rabbit is partially covered with leaves and a few twigs. We prod the rabbit with a stick and see that it's a fresh kill. There's blood near its nose and feet.

Two or three kids hang back and say it's gross. A girl who has a pet rabbit says it's sad. A few of the students talk about how this rabbit will help the bobcat survive. Chris asks the kids what animal covers its kills with leaves and forest debris.

"Bobcat?" says one of the kids.

The student is right, but mountain lions, bears, and fishers also cover their kills. There are no mountain lions here, and black bears are still hibernating. There are no fisher tracks or scat near the rabbit.

"Maybe a bobcat was sitting on that ledge over there and saw the rabbit and snuck up on it," says one of the kids.

"Great guess," says Chris. "And maybe the bobcat that covered up the rabbit will return to feed."

We leave the rabbit because it's time to make our way back to the bus. The group becomes quiet for a moment. I watch the kids watching the faraway ledges, and all of us wonder if there's a bobcat somewhere out there watching us.

BOBCAT FACTS

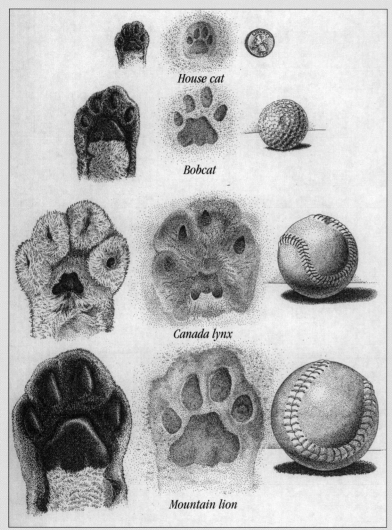

House cat

Bobcat

Canada lynx

Mountain lion

Paws and tracks: a comparison of North American cats

Bobcats *typically weigh between 15 and 30 pounds. Bobcats are bigger than house cats, measuring about 40 inches long from head to tail.*

Lynxes *typically weigh less than bobcats. The lynx has much larger paws; longer legs, fur, and body; and bigger ear tufts than the bobcat.*

Mountain lions *weigh 75 to 200 pounds. Mountain lions have many names, including panther, puma, catamount, and cougar. Their length varies from 6 ½ feet for females to almost 8 feet for males.*

Chapter Four

YOU MAY NEVER SEE A WILD BOBCAT

THIS MOUNTAIN LION HASN'T MOVED for more than 120 years! I'm staring into the eyes of the last cougar shot in Vermont. It was killed in 1881 by a hunter named Alexander Crowell near the town of Barnard, in central Vermont. The lion is displayed at the Vermont Historical Society in Montpelier, Vermont's capital.

The gun that Alexander Crowell used to kill the cat is here, too. After 120 years, this mountain lion still looks impressive. The sign reads that it was the largest catamount on state record, weighing about 182 pounds and measuring 7 feet.

The three members of the felidae, or cat, family in North America are the bobcat, lynx, and mountain lion. The bobcat has the largest range of these three cats. Bobcats are found throughout nearly all of the United States and along the border of Canada. The lynx lives in snow country and is found mostly in Canada, Alaska, the northern Rocky Mountains, as well as northern New England and the upper midwest. A related race of the lynx is also found in Europe, Scandinavia, and Asia. Although mountain lions once lived across North America, today they're found in the western part of the continent, from British Columbia in Canada south to Mexico and South America. A small number of cougars also live in the Florida Everglades where they are very endangered. Occasional confirmed tracks and sightings of cougar have occurred in northern New England and the Berkshires of Massachusetts.

I look at the last mountain lion killed in Vermont and the rifle that killed this beautiful and amazing animal, and I think about America's long war on predators. American settlers saw all predators, including the bobcat, as vermin to be exterminated. During the nineteenth and early-twentieth centuries, the country's view regarding bobcats, cougars, grizzly bears, wolves, and coyotes was simple: The only good predator was a dead predator. Poison, bullets, and traps killed thousands of these animals. Today grizzly bears and wolves are endangered species.

While the bobcat has been hunted and trapped relentlessly for more than two hundred years, this wildcat continues to survive. Biologists estimate there may be as many as

This bobcat was caught in a foot-hold trap in New Mexico around 1931. Thousands of bobcats were killed as a part of the U.S. government's program to destroy predators at the turn of the twentieth century. Today, more than thirty states have a bobcat trapping season.

A rancher killed two bobcats that were preying on his sheep in Nevada around 1925.

BOBCAT FACTS

Habitat specialist and professional tracker Susan Morse of Vermont says, "If we are to keep healthy bobcat and other wildlife populations in the twenty-first century, we need to identify and protect habitat. We not only have to protect big chunks of habitat, but also make sure that that habitat is connected to other large areas of good habitat." Sue worries that increasing human development will threaten wildlife populations. By teaching others how to identify important wildlife habitat, Sue Morse, and the organization she founded called Keeping Track, hopes to protect the homes of future generations of bobcats.

Sue Morse with captive lynx.

750,000 to 1.5 million bobcats in the United States today. Their secret lifestyle and the ability to adapt to many habitats make the bobcats real survivors. By comparison, some western states have several thousand cougars. No one knows for sure how many lynxes exist. The Fish and Wildlife Department has listed the lynx as a "threatened" species in the lower 48 states. Although the bobcat claws out an existence at the beginning of the twenty-first century, it faces the modern threats of human disturbance, vehicles, and habitat loss.

I drive home through Vermont's lush patchwork of woods, mountains, and farmland after my visit to the mounted catamount. I hope this country will always be home for bobcats. I hope there will always be enough rocky ledges where bobcats can hide, enough wetlands where bobcats can hunt, and enough wild forests where bobcats can be bobcats. You and I may never see a wild bobcat, but I want to know they are out there. I want to know there's the possibility that one day while walking a woodland trail I might come around a bend and catch a glimpse of a wide-eyed, spotted cat before it melts into the woods and is gone. I'll never stop looking for them.

INDEX

Further reading:

Bobcats by Caroline Arnold (Lerner Publications, 1997)

Forest Cats of North America by Jerry Kobalenko
(Firefly Books, 1997)

Bobcat Year by Hope Ryden (The Lyons Press, 1990)

Wild Cats by Candace Savage (Sierra Club Books, 1993)